Through the Looking Glass

And What Alice Found There

Lewis Carroll

Condensed and Adapted by
DEBBIE GUTHERY

Illustrated by
JASON ALEXANDER

Cover Illustrated by
PATRICK WHELAN

Dalmatian Press

The Junior Classics have been
adapted and illustrated with care and thought
to introduce you to a world of famous authors, characters, ideas,
and great stories that have been loved for generations.

Editor — Kathryn Knight
Creative Director — Gina Rhodes Haynes
And the entire classics project team
of Dalmatian Publishing Group

THROUGH THE LOOKING GLASS

Copyright © 2012 Dalmatian Press, LLC,
an imprint of Dalmatian Publishing Group.
Franklin, Tennessee 37067 • 1-866-418-2572

ISBN: 1-45305-548-7

Printed in the United States of America

CE12084/0212 CLI

FOREWORD

A note to the reader—

A classic story rests in your hands. The characters are famous. The tale is timeless.

This Junior Classic edition of *Through the Looking Glass* has been carefully condensed and adapted from the original version (which you really *must* read when you're ready for every detail). We kept the well-known phrases for you. We kept Lewis Carroll's style. And we kept the important imagery and heart of the tale.

Literature is terrific fun! It encourages you to think. It helps you dream. It is full of heroes and villains, suspense and humor, adventure and wonder, and new ideas. It introduces you to writers who reach out across time to say: "Do you want to hear a story I wrote?"

Curl up and enjoy.

CONTENTS

CHARACTERS

ALICE — a curious young girl who finds herself on the other side of a mirror in Looking Glass land

BLACK KITTEN — a naughty little kitten who seems to be part of Alice's strange adventures

RED QUEEN — a royal chess piece with plenty of advice for Alice

RED KING — a royal chess piece fond of napping

WHITE QUEEN — a royal chess piece who tends to be a bit "backward" and untidy

WHITE KING — a royal chess piece who writes in a large notebook

TIGER LILY AND ROSE — two of the talking flowers in Looking Glass land

MAN IN WHITE PAPER, GOAT, HORSE, AND GNAT — fellow passengers on the train

ROCKING-HORSEFLY, SNAP-DRAGONFLY, AND BREAD-AND-BUTTERFLY — Looking Glass insects

CHARACTERS

TWEEDLEDUM AND TWEEDLEDEE — odd men who tell Alice about "The Walrus and the Carpenter," and then quarrel over a broken rattle

WALRUS AND THE CARPENTER — two characters in a poem who eat a great many oysters

SHEEP — a knitting shopkeeper who takes Alice for a ride in a rowboat

HUMPTY DUMPTY — a large egghead who explains the "Jabberwocky" poem to Alice, and then has a fall

LION AND THE UNICORN — they fight for the crown and get drummed out of town

HATTA — the King's messenger who enjoys tea

HAIGHA — ("Hayer") the King's other messenger

WHITE KNIGHT — a kind old knight who is very inventive, but tends to fall off his horse

Through the Looking Glass

And What Alice Found There

CHAPTER ONE

Looking Glass House

One thing was certain—the *white* kitten had had nothing to do with it. It was all the black kitten's fault. The white kitten had been having its face washed by its mother, Dinah, for the last fifteen minutes. So you see that it *couldn't* have caused the mischief.

But the black kitten had her bath earlier that afternoon. And so, while Alice was curled up in a corner of the great armchair, half asleep, it played with the ball of yarn that Alice had been trying to wind up. And now the yarn was spread over the hearth rug, in knots and tangles, with the kitten running after its own tail in the middle.

"Oh, you naughty, naughty little thing!" cried Alice as she reached down, scooped up the kitten and the tangled yarn and scrambled back into the armchair. She began winding up the ball again, chatting away, sometimes to the kitten, and sometimes to herself. The kitten sat on her knee, pretending to watch the winding, and now and then it put out one paw and gently touched the ball, as if it would be glad to help.

"I was so angry, Kitty," Alice said, "when I saw the mischief you had done, I was ready to open the window and put you into the snow! And you would have deserved it, you naughty little kitten! What have you got to say for yourself?"

The kitten had nothing to say, so Alice went on. "Kitty, can you play chess? Because, when we were playing just now, you watched as if you understood everything I was doing. And when I said 'Check!' you purred!

"Let's pretend that *you're* the Red Queen, Kitty! I think if you sat up and folded your arms, you'd look exactly like her." Alice got the Red Queen off the table and set it before the kitten. But the kitten would *not* fold its arms, so Alice held the kitten up in front of the looking glass.

"Oh, please try—or I'll put you through into Looking Glass House. How would you like *that*? Now, if you'll just listen, Kitty, and not talk so much, I'll tell you what I think the Looking Glass House is like. If you look through the glass, you'll see that the parlor is just the same as our parlor—only the things go the other way. I can see all of it when I get up on a chair—all of it except what is just behind the fireplace. Oh! I wish I could see *that*! I want to know if they have a fire in the winter. You never *can* tell, unless our fire smokes, and then smoke comes up in *that* room, too. Well, the books are like our books, only the words go the wrong way. I *know* that because I've held up one of our books to the glass, and then they hold one up in the other room.

"Oh, Kitty! How nice it would be if we could get into Looking Glass House! Let's pretend there's a way to get through it." Alice was up on the fireplace mantel when she said this, though she hardly knew how she had got there. Then, like magic, the glass began to melt away, just like a bright silvery mist. In another moment, Alice was through the glass and had jumped lightly down into the Looking Glass room.

The very first thing she did was to look to see if there was a fire in the fireplace, and she was pleased to find that there was one blazing away as brightly as the one she had left behind.

Then she began looking about. Everything seemed to be the same as in the room she had left, but there were very curious differences. The pictures on the wall next to the fire seemed to be alive, and the clock on the mantel had the face of a little old man—and it grinned at her.

"They don't keep this room tidy," Alice thought to herself, as she noticed several of the chessmen down in the fireplace among the cinders. As she looked closer, she was suddenly surprised. The chessmen were walking about, two and two! She got down on her hands and knees to get a better look.

"Here are the Red King and the Red Queen," Alice whispered, for fear of frightening them. "And there are the White King and the White Queen sitting on the edge of the shovel. And here are two Castles walking arm in arm—I don't think they can hear me," she went on, as she moved even closer, "and I'm sure they can't see me. I feel invisible somehow—"

Something began squeaking on the table behind Alice, and she turned just in time to see one of the White Pawns roll over and begin kicking. She watched it with great curiosity to see what would happen next.

"It's my child!" the White Queen cried out as she rushed past the King, so quickly that she knocked him over into the cinders. "My precious Lily! My regal child!" and she began scrambling wildly up the side of the fireplace fender.

"Regal fiddlestick!" said the King, rubbing his nose, which had been hurt by the fall. He had a right to be a *little* annoyed with the Queen, for now he was covered with ashes from head to foot.

Alice was anxious to help, so, as the poor little Lily was having a screaming fit, Alice quickly picked up the Queen and set her on the table by the side of her noisy little daughter.

The Queen gasped, and sat down. The quick journey through the air had taken away her breath. For a minute or two she could do nothing but hug the little Lily in silence. As soon as she had recovered her breath a little, she called out to the White King, who was sitting among the ashes, "Beware of the volcano!"

"What volcano?" said the King, looking up anxiously into the fire, as if he thought that was the most likely place to find one.

"It blew—me—up," panted the Queen, who was still a little out of breath. "Be careful and come up—the regular way—don't get blown up!"

Alice watched the White King as he slowly struggled up the fireplace fender. At last she said, "Why, you'll take hours and hours to get to the table at that rate. I'd better help you, hadn't I?"

So Alice picked him up very gently and lifted him across—very slowly so that she wouldn't take his breath away. But, before she put him on the table, she thought she might as well dust him off a little, since he was covered with ashes.

The King was far too shocked to cry out, but his eyes and his mouth grew larger and larger, and rounder and rounder, until Alice's hand shook so much with laughing that she nearly let him drop upon the floor.

"Oh! *Please* don't make such faces!" she cried out (though he couldn't hear her). "You make me laugh so hard! And close your mouth—the ashes will get into it! There, now—you're tidy enough!" And she set him on the table near the Queen.

The King immediately fell flat on his back and lay perfectly still. Alice was a little alarmed at what she had done, and went round the room to see if she could find any water to throw on him. But, all she could find was a bottle of ink, and when she got back with it she found he had recovered, and he and the Queen were talking together in a whisper—so low that Alice could hardly hear what they said.

The King was saying, "I assure you, my dear, I turned cold to the very ends of my whiskers!"

To which the Queen replied, "You haven't got any whiskers."

"The horror of that moment," the King went on, "I shall never, *never* forget!"

"You will, though," the Queen said, "if you don't make a note of it."

The King took a large notebook out of his pocket and began writing.

There was a book lying near Alice on the table, and while she sat watching the White King, she looked through the pages, to find some part that she could read, "—for it's written in some language I don't know," she said to herself.

It was like this:

JABBERWOCKY
'Twas brillig, and the slithy toves
Did gyre and gimble in the wabe;
All mimsy were the borogoves,
And the mome raths outgrabe.

She puzzled over this for some time, but at last a bright thought struck her. "Why, it's a Looking Glass book, of course! And if I hold it up to a glass, the words will all go the right way again." So she did and this was the poem that Alice read:

JABBERWOCKY
'Twas brillig, and the slithy toves
Did gyre and gimble in the wabe;
All mimsy were the borogoves,
And the mome raths outgrabe.

"Beware the Jabberwock, my son!
The jaws that bite, the claws that catch!
Beware the Jubjub bird, and shun
The frumious Bandersnatch!"

He took his vorpal sword in hand:
Long time the manxome foe he sought—
So rested he by the Tumtum tree,
And stood awhile in thought.

And, as in uffish thought he stood,
The Jabberwock, with eyes of flame,
Came whiffling through the tulgey wood,
And burbled as it came!

One, two! One, two! And through and through
The vorpal blade went snicker-snack!
He left it dead, and with its head
He went galumphing back.

"And hast thou slain the Jabberwock?
Come to my arms, my beamish boy!
O frabjous day! Callooh! Callay!"
He chortled in his joy.

'Twas brillig, and the slithy toves
Did gyre and gimble in the wabe;
All mimsy were the borogoves,
And the mome raths outgrabe.

"It seems very pretty," she said when she had finished it, "but it's *very* hard to understand!" (She didn't want to confess, even to herself, that she didn't understand *any* of it.)

"But oh!" thought Alice, suddenly jumping up. "If I don't hurry, I will have to go back through the Looking Glass before I've seen what the rest of the house is like! Let's have a look at the garden first!"

She was out of the room in a blink, and found herself sliding down the banister, and then floating on through the hall. She caught hold of the doorpost, and was rather glad to find herself walking again in the natural way.

CHAPTER TWO

The Garden of Live Flowers

"I could see the garden much better," said Alice to herself, "if I could get to the top of that hill. And here's a path that leads straight to it—at least, no, it doesn't do *that*, it twists more like a corkscrew than a path! Well, *this* turn goes to the hill, I suppose—no, it doesn't! It goes straight back to the house! Well then, I'll try it the other way."

And so she did. She wandered up and down, and tried turn after turn, but always came back to the house no matter which way she went.

"It's no use talking about it," Alice said, looking up at the house as if it were arguing with her. "I'm *not* finished yet. I know if I go into you,

I'll have to go through the Looking Glass again—back into the old room—and that would be the end of all my adventures!"

So, she turned her back to the house and set out once more down the path, determined to keep straight until she got to the top of the hill. For a few minutes all went well, and just as she was saying, "I really *shall* do it this time—" the path gave a sudden twist and shook itself, and she found herself actually walking back into the door of the house.

"I never saw a house that kept getting in the way! Never!" she cried. However, there was the hill, full in sight, and there was nothing to do but start again. This time she came upon a large flowerbed, with a border of daisies, and a willow tree growing in the middle.

"Oh, Tiger Lily," said Alice to an orange lily waving in the wind, "I *wish* you could talk!"

"We *can* talk," said the Tiger Lily, "when there's anybody worth talking to."

Alice was so surprised that she could not speak for a minute. The Tiger Lily only went on waving about, so Alice spoke again, almost in a whisper. "Can *all* the flowers talk?"

"As well as *you* can," said the Tiger Lily, "and a great deal louder."

"It isn't good manners for us to begin the conversation," said the pink Rose, "and I really was wondering when you'd speak! Your face *has* got some sense, and at least you *do* have the right pinkish color."

"I don't care about the color," the Tiger Lily remarked. "If only her petals curled up a little more, she'd be all right."

"How is it you can all talk?" Alice asked. "I've been in many gardens before, but none of the flowers could talk."

"Put your hand down, and feel the ground," said the Tiger Lily. "Then you'll know why."

Alice did so. "It's very hard," she said, "but I don't see what that has to do with it."

"In most gardens," the Tiger Lily said, "they make the beds too soft—so that the flowers are always asleep."

This sounded like a good reason. "I never thought of that before!" Alice said.

"It's *my* opinion that you never think *at all*," the Rose said in a rather rude tone.

"Hold *your* tongue!" cried the Tiger Lily.

"Are there more people in the garden besides me?" Alice said, ignoring the Rose's last remark.

"There's one other flower in the garden that can move around like you," said the Rose, "but she's more bushy than you are."

"Is she like me?" Alice asked eagerly.

"Well, she has the same shape as you," the Rose said, "but she's redder—and her petals are shorter, I think."

"They're done up close, almost like a dahlia," said the Tiger Lily, "not tumbled about like yours."

"But that's not *your* fault," the Rose added kindly. "You're beginning to fade, so you can't help that your petals are getting a little untidy."

Alice didn't like what they were saying about her, so she changed the subject. "Does she ever come out here?"

"I'm sure you'll see her soon," said the Rose. "She's one of the kind that has nine spikes."

"Where does she wear them?" Alice asked.

"Why, all around her head, of course," the Rose replied. "I was wondering why *you* didn't have some, too."

"She's coming!" cried the Larkspur. "I hear her footstep, thump, thump, along the gravel walk!"

Alice looked around eagerly, and found that it was the Red Queen. "She's grown a good deal!" she remarked. When Alice first found her in the ashes, she had been only three inches high—and here she was, half a head taller than Alice!

"It's the fresh air that does it," said the Rose. "Wonderfully fine air it is, out here."

"I think I'll go and meet her," said Alice. The flowers were interesting, but she felt that it would be much nicer to have a talk with a real Queen.

She soon found herself face to face with the Red Queen, and in sight of the hill she had been trying so hard to get to.

"Where do you come from?" said the Red Queen. "And where are you going? Look up, speak nicely, and don't twiddle your fingers."

Alice followed all these directions and then explained that she had lost her way.

"I don't know what you mean by *your* way," said the Queen. "All the ways here belong to *me*—but why did you come out here at all?" she added in a kinder tone. "Curtsy while you're thinking about what to say. It saves time."

Alice wondered a little at this, but she was too much in awe of the Queen to ask about it.

"It's time for you to answer now," the Queen said, looking at her watch. "Open your mouth a *little* wider when you speak, and always say 'your Majesty.' "

"I only wanted to see what the garden was like, your Majesty—"

"That's perfect," said the Queen, patting her on the head, which Alice didn't like at all. "Though, when you say 'garden'—*I've* seen gardens that would make *these* look like a field."

Alice didn't dare to argue the point, but went on, "—and I thought I'd try and find my way to the top of that hill—"

"When you say 'hill,' " the Queen interrupted, "*I* could show you hills that would make you call *that* hill a valley."

"A hill *can't* be a valley, you know," said Alice, surprised that she was arguing with her. "That would be nonsense—"

The Red Queen shook her head. "You may call it 'nonsense' if you like," she said, "but *I've* heard nonsense that would make *that* sound as sensible as a dictionary!"

Alice curtsied again, and they walked in silence until they got to the top of the little hill.

For some minutes Alice didn't speak. She looked out in all directions over the country—and what a curious country it was. There were many tiny little brooks running straight across it from side to side. The ground between was divided up into squares by little green hedges.

"I declare it looks like a large chessboard!" Alice said at last, quite delighted. "There ought to be some chessmen moving around somewhere—and there they are!" Her heart began to beat quickly with excitement. "It's a great huge game of chess that's being played! Oh, how I *wish* I were one of the players! I wouldn't mind being a Pawn, if I could join—though of course I would *like* to be a Queen most of all." She glanced rather shyly at the real Queen as she said this.

The Queen only smiled pleasantly and said, "That's easily done. You can be the White Queen's Pawn, if you like, since Lily's too young to play. You're in the Second Square to begin with. When you get to the Eighth Square you'll be a Queen—"

Just at that moment, they began to run! And the Queen was crying "Faster! Faster!", but Alice felt she *could not* go faster, though she was too out of breath to say so.

The curious thing was that the trees and the other things around them never changed their places at all. No matter how fast they ran, they never seemed to pass anything. "I wonder if all the things move along with us?" thought poor, puzzled Alice.

The Queen seemed to read her mind, for she cried, "Faster! Don't try to talk!"

"Are we nearly there?" Alice managed to pant out at last.

"Nearly there?" the Queen repeated. "Why, we passed it ten minutes ago! Faster!" And they skimmed through the air for a time in silence, with the wind whistling in Alice's ears, and almost blowing her hair off her head, so she thought.

Then suddenly, just as Alice was getting quite exhausted, they stopped, and she found herself sitting on the ground, breathless and giddy.

The Queen propped her up against a tree, and said, "You may rest a little now."

Alice looked around her in great surprise. "Why, I do believe we've been under this tree the whole time! Everything's just as it was!"

"Of course it is," said the Queen. "Why wouldn't it be?"

"Well, in *our* country," said Alice, still panting a little, "you'd get to somewhere else—if you ran very fast for a long time, as we've been doing."

"A slow sort of country!" said the Queen. "Now, *here* it takes all the running you can *do*, to keep in the same place. If you want to get somewhere else, you must run at least twice as fast as that!"

"I'd rather not try, please!" said Alice. "I'm quite content to stay here—only I *am* so hot and thirsty!"

"I know what *you'd* like!" the Queen said. She took a little box out of her pocket. "Have a biscuit?"

Alice thought it would not be good manners to say "No," though it wasn't at all what she wanted. So she took it and ate it. It was *very* dry and she thought she might choke trying to swallow it down with nothing to drink.

"While you're refreshing yourself," said the Queen, "I'll just take the measurements."

She took a ribbon out of her pocket, marked in inches, and began measuring the ground and sticking little pegs in here and there.

"At the end of two yards," the Queen said, putting a peg into the ground, "I shall give you your directions—have another biscuit?"

"No, thank you. One is *quite* enough!" said Alice.

"Thirst quenched, I hope?" said the Queen.

Alice wasn't sure how to reply—but the Queen didn't wait for her answer and kept on speaking.

"Now, at the end of *three* yards I shall repeat the directions—in case you forget them. At the end of *four* yards, I shall say good-bye. And at the end of *five*, I shall go!"

When she had finished placing all the pegs in the ground, she returned to the tree and slowly began walking back down the row. Alice was very interested in what she would do.

At the two-yard peg, she turned around and said, "A pawn can move two squares in its first move, you know. So you'll go *very* quickly through the Third Square—by railway, I should think. You'll find yourself in the Fourth Square in no time. Well, *that* square belongs to Tweedledum and Tweedledee. The Fifth is mostly water. The Sixth belongs to Humpty Dumpty—" The Queen paused. "Why have you said nothing?"

"I—I didn't know I had to," Alice said.

"You *should* have said, 'It's extremely kind of you to tell me all this'—however, we'll suppose you did. The Seventh Square is all forest—however, one of the Knights will show you the way. And in the Eighth Square we shall be Queens together, and it's all feasting and fun!"

Alice got up and curtsied, and sat down again.

At the next peg, the Queen turned again and said, "Speak in French when you can't think of the English for a thing—turn out your toes as you walk—and remember who you are." Then she walked to the next peg, said "Good-bye," and hurried on to the last peg.

How it happened Alice never knew—but just as the Red Queen came to the last peg, she was gone. And Alice remembered that she was a Pawn, and that it would soon be time for her to make her first move.

CHAPTER THREE

Looking Glass Insects

Of course, the first thing to do was to look around the country she was going to travel through. "It's like learning geography," thought Alice, as she stood on tiptoe in hopes of being able to see a little farther. She looked for rivers and mountains and towns—and saw none—but then something caught Alice's eye.

"Why, what *are* those creatures, making honey down there? They can't be bees—nobody ever saw bees a mile off—" and for some time she stood silent, watching one of them bustling about among the flowers, poking its long nose into them, "just as if it was a regular bee," thought Alice.

However, this was anything but a regular bee. In fact it was an elephant—as Alice soon found out. "And what enormous flowers they must be!" was her next thought. "What a large amount of honey they must make! I think I'll go down and—no, I won't go *just* yet," she went on. "I think I'll go down the other way, and perhaps I may visit the elephants later on. Besides, I *do* so want to get into the Third Square!"

So with this excuse, she ran down the hill and jumped over the first of the six little brooks.

"Tickets, please!" said the Guard, putting his head in at the window. In a moment everybody was holding out a ticket. They were about the same size as the people, and seemed to fill the carriage.

"Now then! Show your ticket, child!" the Guard went on, looking at Alice. And a great many voices all said together, just like a chorus, "Don't keep him waiting, child! Why, his time is worth a thousand pounds a minute!"

"I'm afraid I haven't got one," Alice said in a frightened tone. "There wasn't a ticket office where I came from."

And again the chorus of voices went on. "There wasn't room for one where she came from. The land there is worth a thousand pounds an inch!"

"Don't make excuses," said the Guard. "You should have bought one from the engine driver." He stood looking at her—first through a telescope, then through a microscope, and then through an opera glass. At last he said, "You're traveling the wrong way," and shut up the window and went away.

"So young a child," said the gentleman sitting across from her (he was dressed in white paper), "ought to know which way she's going, even if she doesn't know her own name!"

A Goat, that was sitting next to the gentleman in white, shut his eyes and said in a loud voice, "She ought to know her way to the ticket office, even if she doesn't know her alphabet!"

There was a Beetle sitting next to the Goat, and *he* said, "She'll have to go back from here as luggage!"

Alice couldn't see who was sitting beyond the Beetle, but a hoarse voice spoke next. "Change engines—" it said, and there it choked up.

"It sounds like a horse," Alice thought to herself. And an extremely small voice close to her ear said, "You might make a joke on that—something about 'horse' and 'hoarse,' you know."

And after that, other voices went on, saying what Alice ought to do. But the gentleman dressed in white paper leaned forward and whispered in her ear, "Never mind what they all say, my dear, but take a return ticket every time the train stops."

"I will not!" Alice said rather impatiently. "I don't belong to this railway at all—I was in some woods just now and I wish I could get back there."

"You might make a joke on that," said the little voice close to her ear. "Something about 'you would if you could,' you know."

"Don't tease me so," said Alice, looking around to see where the voice came from. "If you want to have a joke made, why don't you make one yourself?"

The little voice sighed deeply. "I know you are a friend," it said, "a dear friend, and an old friend. And you won't hurt me, though I am an insect."

"What kind of insect?" Alice asked nervously. What she really wanted to know was whether it could sting or not.

"What, then you don't—" the little voice began, when it was drowned out by a shrill scream from the engine. Everybody jumped up in alarm.

The Horse looked out the window, then quietly said, "It's only a brook we have to jump over."

No one seemed bothered by this, though Alice felt a little nervous at the idea of trains jumping. "But it will take us into the Fourth Square!" she said to herself. She felt the carriage rise straight up into the air, and in her fright she caught at the thing nearest to her hand, which happened to be the Goat's beard.

But the beard seemed to melt away, and she found herself sitting quietly under a tree. The Gnat (that was the insect she had been talking to) was balancing itself on a twig just over her head, and fanning her with its wings.

It certainly was a *very* large Gnat, "about the size of a chicken," Alice thought. Still, she wasn't nervous—they *had* been talking together so long.

"—then you don't like *all* insects?" the Gnat went on, as quietly as if nothing had happened.

"I like them when they can talk," Alice said. "None of them ever talk, where *I* come from."

"What sort of insects do you rejoice in, where *you* come from?" the Gnat asked.

"I don't rejoice in insects at all," Alice explained, "because I'm afraid of them—at least the large kinds. But I can tell you the names of some of them."

"Do they answer to their names?" the Gnat asked.

"I never knew them to do it."

"In the woods down there, they've got no names—however, go on with your list of insects. You're wasting time."

"Well, there's the Horsefly," Alice began, counting off the names on her fingers.

"All right," said the Gnat. "Halfway up that bush, you'll see a Rocking-Horsefly, if you look. It's made entirely of wood, and moves around by swinging itself from branch to branch."

"What does it eat?" Alice asked, with great curiosity.

"Sap and sawdust," said the Gnat. "Go on with the list."

Alice looked up at the Rocking-Horsefly with great interest, and made up her mind that it must have been just repainted, it looked so bright and sticky.

"And there's the Dragonfly," Alice said.

"Look on the branch above your head," said the Gnat, "and there you'll find a Snap-Dragonfly. Its body is made of plum pudding, its wings of holly leaves, and its head is a raisin burning in brandy."

"And what does *it* eat?"

"Frumenty and mince pie," the Gnat replied, "and it makes its nest in a Christmas box."

"And then there's the Butterfly," Alice went on.

"Crawling at your feet," said the Gnat, "you may observe a Bread-and-Butterfly. Its wings are slices of bread-and-butter, its body is crust, and its head is a lump of sugar."

"And what does *it* live on?"

"Weak tea with cream in it."

Alice was silent for a minute or two, thinking. The Gnat amused itself by humming around her head. At last it settled again and remarked, "I suppose you don't want to lose your name?"

"No, indeed," Alice said, a little anxiously.

"And yet I don't know…" the Gnat went on. "How convenient it would be if you could manage to go home without it! For instance, if the nanny called you to do your lessons, she would call out 'Come here—' and then she would pause, because there wouldn't be any name for her to call, and of course you wouldn't have to go, you know."

"That would never do, I'm sure," said Alice. "The nanny would never think of excusing me from lessons for that. If she couldn't remember my name, she'd call me 'Miss!' "

"Well, if she said 'Miss,' and didn't say anything more," the Gnat said, "of course you'd miss your lessons. That's a joke. I wish *you* had made it."

"Why do you wish *I* had made it?" Alice asked. "It's a very bad joke."

But the Gnat only sighed and two large tears rolled down its cheeks.

"You shouldn't make jokes," Alice said, "if it makes you so unhappy."

Then came another sad little sigh, and this time the poor Gnat really seemed to have sighed itself away, for, when Alice looked up, there was nothing to be seen on the twig. So she got up and walked on.

Soon she came to an open field, with woods on the other side of it. It looked much darker than the last woods, and Alice felt a *little* nervous about going into it. But she made up her mind to go on. It was, after all, the only way to the Eighth Square.

"These must be the woods," she said to herself, "where things have no names. I wonder what'll become of *my* name when I go in? I wouldn't like to lose it at all—because they'd have to give me another, and it would be almost certain to be an ugly one. But it would be fun trying to find the creature that had got my old name!"

She reached the woods. It looked very cool and shady. "Well, at least it's a great comfort," she said as she stepped under the trees, "after being so hot, to get into the—into the—into *what*?" she tried to go on but she was unable to think of the word she needed. "I mean to get under the—under the—under *this*, you know!" putting her hand on the trunk of the tree. "What *does* it call itself, I wonder? I do believe it's got no name—why, to be sure it hasn't!"

She stood silent for a minute, thinking. "It really *has* happened, after all! And now, who am I? L… I *know* it begins with L!"

Just then a Fawn came wandering by. It looked at Alice with its large gentle eyes, but didn't seem at all frightened. She held out her hand and tried to stroke it—but it only stepped back a little, and then stood looking at her again.

"What do you call yourself?" the Fawn said at last.

"I wish I knew!" thought poor Alice. She answered, "Nothing, just now."

"Think again," it said.

Alice thought, but nothing came of it. "Please, would you tell me what *you* call *yourself*?" she said timidly. "I think that might help a little."

"I'll tell you, if you'll move a little further on," the Fawn said. "I can't remember *here*."

So they walked on together through the woods, Alice with her arms clasped lovingly around the soft neck of the Fawn, until they came out into another open field. The Fawn suddenly bounded into the air, and shook itself free from Alice's arms. "I'm a Fawn!" it cried out in a voice of delight. "And, dear me! You're a human child!" A sudden look of alarm came into its beautiful brown eyes, and it darted away at full speed.

Alice stood looking after it, almost ready to cry with having lost her dear little fellow traveler so suddenly.

"However, I know my name now," she said. "Alice—Alice—I won't forget it again."

Just in front of her there were two sign posts pointing the same way, one marked "TO TWEEDLEDUM'S HOUSE" and the other "TO THE HOUSE OF TWEEDLEDEE."

"I do believe," said Alice, "that they live in the *same* house! I'll just call and say 'How d'you do?' and ask them the way out of the woods. If I could only get to the Eighth Square before it gets dark!"

So she wandered on, talking to herself as she went, until she turned a sharp corner and she came upon two fat little men, so suddenly that she could not help being startled. But she pulled herself together, feeling sure that they must be—

CHAPTER FOUR

Tweedledum and Tweedledee

They were standing under a tree, each with an arm around the other's neck. Alice knew which was which in a moment, because one of them had "DUM" stitched on his collar, and the other had "DEE." "I suppose they've got 'TWEEDLE' stitched at the back of their collars," she said to herself.

They stood so still that she forgot they were alive. She was just about to look at the back of each collar for "TWEEDLE" when she was startled by a voice coming from the one marked "DUM."

"If you think we're made out of wax," he said, "you ought to pay, you know. Waxworks weren't made to be looked at for nothing, nohow!"

"Contrariwise," added the one marked "DEE," "if you think we're alive, you should speak."

"I'm very sorry," was all Alice could say, but the old song kept ringing through her head:

> *Tweedledum and Tweedledee*
> *Agreed to have a battle;*
> *For Tweedledum said Tweedledee*
> *Had spoiled his nice new rattle.*

> *Just then flew down a monstrous crow,*
> *As black as a tar barrel;*
> *Which frightened both the heroes so,*
> *They quite forgot their quarrel.*

"I know what you're thinking about," said Tweedledum, "but it isn't so, nohow."

"Contrariwise," continued Tweedledee, "if it was so, it might be. And if it were so, it would be. But as it isn't, it ain't. That's logic."

"I was thinking," Alice said very politely, "which is the best way out of these woods. It's getting so dark. Would you tell me, please?"

But the fat little men only looked at each other and grinned.

"You've begun wrong!" cried Tweedledum.

"The first thing in a visit is to say 'How d'ye do?' and shake hands!" And the two brothers gave each other a hug. Then they held out the two hands that were free, to shake hands with Alice.

Alice did not like shaking hands with either of them first, for fear of hurting the other one's feelings. So, she took hold of both hands at once. The next moment, they were dancing round in a ring, and Alice found herself singing: *Here we go round the mulberry bush.* This seemed quite natural, "But it certainly *was* funny," she thought.

The other two dancers were fat, and soon out of breath. "Four times around is enough for one dance," Tweedledum panted out, and stopped dancing as suddenly as they had begun. Then they let go of Alice's hands, and stood looking at her for a minute.

"I hope you're not too tired?" she said at last.

"Nohow. And thank you *very* much for asking," said Tweedledum.

"So much obliged!" added Tweedledee. "You like poetry?"

"Ye-es—*some* poetry," Alice said hesitantly. "But would you please tell me which road leads out of the woods?"

"What shall I recite to her?" said Tweedledee, looking round at Tweedledum with great solemn eyes, and not noticing Alice's question.

"*The Walrus and the Carpenter* is longest," Tweedledum replied, giving his brother a hug.

Tweedledee began instantly:

The sun was shining—

Alice interrupted. "If it's *very* long," she said, as politely as she could, "would you please tell me first which road—"

Tweedledee smiled gently, and began again:

> *The sun was shining on the sea,*
> *Shining with all his might.*
> *He did his very best to make*
> *The billows smooth and bright—*
> *And this was odd, because it was*
> *The middle of the night.*

> *The moon was shining sulkily,*
> *Because she thought the sun*
> *Had got no business to be there*
> *After the day was done—*
> *"It's very rude of him," she said,*
> *"To come and spoil the fun!"*

The sea was wet as wet could be,
The sands were dry as dry.
You could not see a cloud, because
No cloud was in the sky:
No birds were flying over head—
There were no birds to fly.

The Walrus and the Carpenter
Were walking close at hand.
They wept like anything to see
Such quantities of sand.
"If this were only cleared away,"
They said, "it would be grand!"

"If seven maids with seven mops
Swept it for half a year,
Do you suppose," the Walrus said,
"That they could get it clear?"
"I doubt it," said the Carpenter,
And shed a bitter tear.

"O Oysters, come and walk with us!"
The Walrus did beseech.
"A pleasant walk, a pleasant talk,
Along the briny beach.
We cannot do with more than four,
To give a hand to each."

The eldest Oyster looked at him,
But never a word he said.
The eldest Oyster winked his eye,
And shook his heavy head—
Meaning to say he did not choose
To leave the oyster bed.

But four young oysters hurried up,
All eager for the treat.
Their coats were brushed, their faces washed,
Their shoes were clean and neat—
And this was odd, because, you know,
They hadn't any feet.

Four other Oysters followed them,
And yet another four;
And thick and fast they came at last,
And more, and more, and more—
All hopping through the frothy waves,
And scrambling to the shore.

The Walrus and the Carpenter
Walked on a mile or so,
And then they rested on a rock
Conveniently low.
And all the little Oysters stood
And waited in a row.

"The time has come," the Walrus said,
    "To talk of many things:
Of shoes—and ships—and sealing-wax—
    Of cabbages—and kings—
And why the sea is boiling hot—
    And whether pigs have wings."

"But wait a bit," the Oysters cried,
    "Before we have our chat;
For some of us are out of breath,
    And all of us are fat!"
"No hurry!" said the Carpenter.
    They thanked him much for that.

"A *loaf of bread*," the Walrus said,
"Is what we chiefly need.
Pepper and vinegar besides
Are very good indeed—
Now if you're ready, Oysters dear,
We can begin to feed."

"But not on us!" the Oysters cried,
Turning a little blue.
"After such kindness, that would be
A dismal thing to do!"
"The night is fine," the Walrus said.
"Do you admire the view?

"It was so kind of you to come!
And you are very nice!"
The Carpenter said nothing but
"Cut us another slice.
I wish you were not quite so deaf—
I've had to ask you twice!"

"It seems a shame," the Walrus said,
"To play them such a trick,
After we've brought them out so far,
And made them trot so quick!"
The Carpenter said nothing but
"The butter's spread too thick!"

"I weep for you," the Walrus said.
"I deeply sympathize."
With sobs and tears he sorted out
Those of the largest size,
Holding his pocket handkerchief
Before his streaming eyes.

"O Oysters," said the Carpenter,
"You've had a pleasant run!
Shall we be trotting home again?"
But answer came there none—
And that was scarcely odd, because
They'd eaten every one.

"I like the Walrus best," said Alice, "because, you see, he was a *little* sorry for the poor oysters."

"He ate more than the Carpenter, though," said Tweedledee. "You see, he held his handkerchief in front, so that the Carpenter couldn't count how many he took. Contrariwise."

"That was mean!" Alice said. "Then I like the Carpenter best—if he didn't eat as many as the Walrus."

"But he ate as many as he could get," said Tweedledum.

This was a puzzler. "Well! They were *both* very unpleasant characters—" Here she was alarmed by something that sounded to her like the puffing of a large steam engine in the woods near them. She was afraid it was a wild beast. "Are there any lions or tigers about here?" she asked timidly.

"It's only the Red King snoring," said Tweedledee.

"Come and look at him!" both the brothers cried, and they each took one of Alice's hands, and led her up to where the King was sleeping.

"Isn't he a lovely sight?" said Tweedledum.

He had a tall red nightcap on, with a tassel, and he was lying crumpled up into an untidy heap, and snoring loudly.

"I'm afraid he'll catch cold lying on the damp grass," said Alice, who was a thoughtful little girl.

"He's dreaming now," said Tweedledee, "and what do you think he's dreaming about?"

Alice said, "Nobody can guess that."

"Why, about *you*!" Tweedledee exclaimed, clapping his hands. "And if he *stopped* dreaming about you, where do you suppose you'd be?"

"Where I am now, of course," said Alice.

"Not you!" Tweedledee snapped. "You'd be nowhere. Why, you're only a thing in his dream!"

"If that there King was to wake," Tweedledum added, "you'd go out—bang!—just like a candle!"

"I would not!" Alice exclaimed. "Besides, if *I'm* only a thing in his dream, what are *you*, I should like to know?"

"Ditto," said Tweedledum.

"Ditto, ditto," shouted Tweedledee.

"Hush! You'll wake him," said Alice. "I'd better be getting out of the woods, for it's getting dark. Do you think it's going to rain?"

Tweedledum opened a large umbrella over himself and his brother, and looked up into it. "No, I don't think it is," he said. "At least—not under *here*. Nohow."

"But it may rain *outside*?"

"It may—if it chooses," said Tweedledee. "We've no objection. Contrariwise."

"Selfish things!" thought Alice. She was just going to say "Good-night" when Tweedledum sprang out from under the umbrella.

"Do you see *that*?" he said as his eyes grew large. He pointed a trembling finger at a small white thing lying under a tree.

"It's only a rattle," Alice said, "—only an old rattle—quite old and broken."

"I knew it was!" cried Tweedledum. He stamped about wildly and tore at his hair. "It's spoiled, of course!" He looked at Tweedledee, who was trying to hide under the umbrella.

Alice tried to soothe him. "You needn't be so angry about an old rattle."

"But it isn't old!" Tweedledum cried in a fury. "It's new, I tell you—my nice NEW RATTLE!" Then he looked at Tweedledee and calmly asked, "Of course you agree to have a battle?"

"I suppose so," said Tweedledee.

The two brothers went off hand-in-hand and returned with blankets, pillows, rugs, and coal buckets—and Alice helped them dress for battle.

Alice thought they were quite silly. It took so long to get bundled up in their blankets and helmets that Tweedledum suggested, "Let's just fight till six o'clock, and then have dinner."

"Very well," said the other. "*She* can watch."

"And all this fuss about a rattle!" said Alice.

"There's only one sword, you know," said Tweedledum to Tweedledee, "but *you* can have the umbrella—it's quite sharp. Only we must begin quick. It's getting as dark as can be."

"And darker," said Tweedledee.

It was getting dark so suddenly that Alice thought there must be a thunderstorm coming on. "What a thick black cloud that is!" she said. "And how fast it comes! Why, I do believe it's got wings!"

"It's the crow!" Tweedledum cried out in a shrill voice of alarm. The two brothers took to their heels and were soon out of sight.

Alice ran a little way into the woods, and stopped under a large tree. "It can never get at me *here*," she thought. "It's far too large to squeeze itself in among the trees. I wish it wouldn't flap its wings so hard—it makes it quite windy in the woods—Oh! There's somebody's shawl being blown away!"

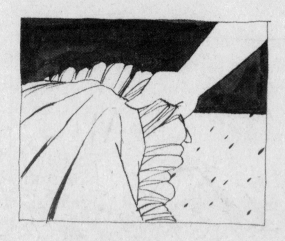

CHAPTER FIVE

Wool and Water

She caught the shawl and looked about for the owner. Soon, the White Queen came running wildly through the woods, with both arms stretched out wide, as if she were flying, and Alice went to meet her with the shawl.

"I'm very glad I happened to be in the way," Alice said. She helped her put on her shawl again.

The White Queen only looked at her and whispered, "Bread-and-butter, bread-and-butter."

Alice asked the White Queen timidly, "*Am* I addressing the White Queen?"

"Well, yes, if you call that a-dressing," the Queen said. "It isn't *my* idea of a-dressing."

"If your Majesty will only tell me the right way to address you, I'll do it the best that I can."

"But I don't want it done at all!" groaned the poor Queen. "I've been a-dressing myself for the last two hours."

"But everything's crooked," thought Alice, "with pins sticking out all over." She added aloud, "May I put your shawl on straight for you?"

"I don't know what's the matter with it!" the Queen said. "It's not behaving, I guess. I've pinned it here, and I've pinned it there, but there's no pleasing it!"

"It *can't* go straight, if you pin it all on one side," Alice said, as she gently fixed it for her. "And, dear me, what a mess your hair is!"

"The brush has got entangled in it!" the Queen said with a sigh. "And I lost the comb yesterday."

Alice carefully released the brush and fixed her hair nicely. "You look much better now," she said, "but really you should have a lady's-maid."

"I'm sure *you'll* do just fine!" the Queen said. "Two pennies a week, and jam every other day."

Alice couldn't help laughing. "I don't want you to hire *me*—and I don't care for jam."

"It's very good jam," said the Queen.

"Well, I don't want any *today*."

"You couldn't have it if you *did* want it," the Queen said. "The rule is: jam tomorrow and jam yesterday—but never jam *today*."

"It *must* come sometimes to 'jam today.' "

"No, it can't," said the Queen. "It's jam every *other* day. Today isn't any *other* day, you know."

"I don't understand. It's confusing!" said Alice.

"That's what it is like living backwards," the Queen said kindly. "It always makes one feel a little strange at first—"

"Living backwards!" Alice repeated. "I never heard of such a thing!"

"—but there's one great advantage in it—that one's memory works both ways."

"I'm sure *mine* only works one way," Alice remarked. "I can't remember things before they happen. What do *you* remember best?"

"Oh, things that happened the week after next. For instance," the Queen went on, putting a large bandage on her finger as she spoke, "there's the King's Messenger. He's in prison now—being punished. And the trial doesn't even *begin* till next Wednesday. Of course, the crime will happen last of all, and—and—" Her voice became a squeak.

Alice was just about to say, "That can't be right—" when the Queen started to scream so loud that she could not finish her sentence.

"Oh, oh, oh!" shouted the Queen, shaking her hand about as if she wanted to shake it off. "My finger's bleeding! Oh, oh, oh, oh!" Her screams were so much like the whistle of a steam engine that Alice had to hold both her hands over her ears.

"What *is* the matter?" Alice said, as soon as there was a chance of making herself heard. "Have you pricked your finger?"

"I haven't pricked it *yet*," the Queen said, "but I soon shall—oh, oh, oh!"

"When do you expect to do it?" Alice asked, feeling like laughing.

"When I fasten my shawl again," the poor Queen groaned, "the brooch will come undone. Oh, oh!" As she said the words the brooch flew open, and the Queen clutched wildly at it, and tried to clasp it again.

"Be careful!" cried Alice. "You're holding it all crooked!" And she reached for the brooch, but it was too late—the pin had slipped, and the Queen had pricked her finger.

"That is why I am bleeding, you see," she said to Alice with a smile. "Now you understand the way things happen here."

"But why don't you scream *now*?" Alice asked, holding her hands ready to put over her ears again.

"Why, I've done all the screaming already," said the Queen. "What would be the good of having it all over again?"

By this time it was starting to get light. "The crow must have flown away, I think," said Alice. "I'm so glad it's gone. I thought it was the night coming on."

"I wish *I* could manage to be glad!" the Queen said. "Only I never can remember the rule. You must be happy, being so glad. How old are you?"

"I'm seven and a half, exactly."

"You needn't say 'exactually,' " the Queen said. "I can believe it without that. Now I'll give *you* something to believe. I'm just one hundred and one, five months and a day."

"I can't believe *that*!" said Alice.

"Can't you?" the Queen said. "Try again. Draw a long breath, and shut your eyes."

Alice laughed. "There's no use trying," she said. "I *can't* believe impossible things."

"I daresay you haven't had much practice," said the Queen. "When I was your age, I always did it for half-an-hour each day. Why, sometimes I've believed as many as six impossible things before breakfast. Oh! There goes the shawl again!"

The brooch had come undone and a sudden gust of wind blew the Queen's shawl across a little brook. The Queen spread out her arms again, and went flying after it. "I've got it!" she cried. "Now you shall see me pin it on again, all by myself!"

"Then I hope your finger is better now?" Alice said very politely, as she crossed the little brook after the Queen.

"Oh, much better!" cried the Queen, her voice rising to a squeak as she went on. "Much be-etter! Be-etter! Be-e-e-etter! Be-e-ehh!" The last word ended in a long bleat, so much like a sheep that Alice was startled.

She looked at the Queen, who seemed to have suddenly wrapped herself up in wool.

Alice rubbed her eyes, and looked again. Was she in a little dark shop? And was that really a sheep with glasses that was sitting on the other side of the counter—knitting?

"What is it you want to buy?" the Sheep said at last, looking up from her knitting.

"I don't know yet," Alice said very gently. "I would like to look all around first, if I might."

"You may look in front of you, and on both sides, if you like," said the Sheep, "but you can't look *all* around you—unless you've got eyes at the back of your head."

Alice did not have eyes in the back of her head, so she kept turning around and around, looking at the shelves as she came to them.

The shop was full of curious things—but the oddest part of it all was that whenever Alice looked hard at any shelf, to see what was on it, that particular shelf was always empty, but the other shelves around it were quite full.

"Things sure do change quickly here!" she said. She had spent a minute or so chasing a large bright thing, that looked sometimes like a doll and sometimes like a workbox—and seemed to keep moving to the next highest shelf.

"Are you a child or a spinning top?" the Sheep said, as she picked up another pair of needles. "You'll make me dizzy soon, if you go on turning around like that." She was now working with fourteen pairs at once, and Alice couldn't help looking at her in great astonishment.

"How *can* she knit with so many?" Alice thought to herself. "She looks like a porcupine."

"Can you row?" the Sheep asked, handing her a pair of knitting needles as she spoke.

"Yes, a little—but not on land—and not with needles—" Alice was beginning to say—

—when suddenly the needles turned into oars in her hands and she found they were in a little boat, gliding along between the banks of a river.

"You'll be catching a crab soon," said the Sheep.

"A dear little crab!" thought Alice. "I would like that. Please tell me, where *are* the crabs?"

"In the water, of course!" The Sheep picked up several more needles and stuck some in her hair.

The boat glided gently through tangled weeds. Alice did her best at rowing as she looked about. She caught sight of some lovely water-grass, and cried out in delight, "Oh, please! There are some scented rushes!"

"You needn't say 'please' to *me* about 'em," the Sheep said, without looking up from her knitting. "I didn't put 'em there, and I'm not going to take 'em away."

"No, but I meant—please, may we pick some?" Alice pleaded. "If you don't mind stopping the boat for a minute."

"How am *I* to stop it?" said the Sheep. "If you stop rowing, it'll stop of itself."

Alice stopped rowing and the boat drifted down the stream until it glided gently in among the waving rushes. Alice pushed up her sleeves and plunged her arms into the water to get hold of the rushes. And for a while Alice forgot all about the Sheep and the knitting. She bent over the side of the boat, with just the ends of her tangled hair dipping into the water—while with bright eager eyes she caught at one bunch after another of the darling scented rushes.

"I hope the boat won't tipple over!" she said to herself. "Oh, *what* a lovely one! Only I can't quite reach it," she said at last, with a sigh. And with flushed cheeks and dripping hair and hands, she scrambled back into her place, and began to arrange her new-found treasures.

They hadn't gone much farther when one of the oars got stuck in the water and *wouldn't* come out again. The handle of it was caught under her chin and it swept Alice straight off the seat, and down into the heap of rushes.

The Sheep went on with her knitting, just as if nothing had happened. "That was a nice crab you caught!" she remarked, as Alice got back into her place, very much relieved to find herself still in the boat.

"Was it? I didn't see it," said Alice, peeping over the side of the boat into the dark water. "I wish it hadn't let go—I would like to see a little crab to take home with me!" But the Sheep only laughed, and went on with her knitting.

"Are there many crabs here?" asked Alice.

"Crabs, and all sorts of things," said the Sheep. "Plenty of choices, only make up your mind. Now, what *do* you want to buy?"

"To buy?" Alice echoed in confusion, for the oars, and the boat, and the river, had vanished, and she was back in the little dark shop.

"I would like to buy an egg, please," she said timidly. "How do you sell them?"

"Fivepence farthing for one—twopence for two," the Sheep replied.

"Then two are cheaper than one?" Alice said in a surprised tone, taking out her purse.

"Only you *must* eat them both, if you buy two," said the Sheep.

"Then I'll have *one*, please," said Alice, as she put the money down on the counter. "After all," she thought, "they may not be very tasty."

The Sheep took the money, and put it away in a box. Then she said, "I never put things into people's hands—that would never do—you must get it for yourself." And she went off to the other end of the shop, and set the egg on a shelf.

"I wonder *why* it wouldn't do?" thought Alice. She made her way among the tables and chairs, for the shop was very dark toward the end. "The egg seems to get further away the more I walk toward it. Let me see, is this a chair? Why, it's got branches, I declare! How very odd to find trees growing here! And actually here's a little brook! Well, this is the most curious shop I ever saw!"

So she went on, as everything turned into a tree the moment she came up to it—and she quite expected the egg to do the same.

CHAPTER SIX

Humpty Dumpty

However, the egg only grew larger and larger, and more and more human. When she had come closer to it, she saw it had eyes and a nose and mouth. And when she had come still closer to it, she saw clearly that it was HUMPTY DUMPTY himself. "It can't be anybody else!" she said to herself.

Humpty Dumpty was sitting, with his legs crossed, on the top of a high, narrow wall. His eyes stared off, as if he didn't notice her. She thought he must be a stuffed figure.

"He's exactly like an egg!" she said aloud, standing with her hands ready to catch him, expecting him to fall at any moment.

"It's *very* frustrating," Humpty Dumpty said after a long silence, looking away from Alice as he spoke, "to be called an egg—*very!*"

"I said you *looked* like an egg, sir," Alice explained. "And some eggs are very pretty, you know," she added, hoping to turn her remark into a compliment.

"Some people," said Humpty Dumpty, looking away from her, "have no more sense than a baby!"

Alice didn't know what to say to this. It wasn't at all like a real conversation. He never looked at her when he spoke. In fact, his last remark was spoken to the tree—so she stood and softly repeated to herself—

Humpty Dumpty sat on a wall.
Humpty Dumpty had a great fall.
All the King's horses and all the King's men
Couldn't put Humpty Dumpty in his place again.

"That last line is much too long," she added out loud, forgetting Humpty Dumpty would hear her.

"Don't stand there chattering to yourself like that," Humpty Dumpty said, looking at her for the first time. "Tell me your name and business."

"My *name* is Alice, but—"

"That's a silly name!" Humpty Dumpty interrupted. "What does it mean?"

"*Must* a name mean something?" Alice asked.

"Of course it must," Humpty Dumpty said with a short laugh. "*My* name means the shape I am. With a name like Alice, you might be any shape."

"Why do you sit out here alone?" said Alice, not wishing to begin an argument.

"Why, because there's nobody with me!" cried Humpty Dumpty. "Did you think I didn't know the answer to *that*? Ask another."

"Don't you think you'd be safer down on the ground?" Alice went on. "That wall is *very* narrow!"

"What easy riddles you ask!" Humpty Dumpty growled out. "Of course I don't think so! Why, if ever I *did* fall off—which there's no chance of—but *if* I did—" He pursed up his lips to look grand. "*If* I *did* fall, *the King has promised me—The King has promised me—with his very own mouth—to—to—*"

"To send all his horses and all his men," Alice interrupted, rather foolishly.

"You've been listening at doors—and behind trees—and down chimneys—or you couldn't have known it!" Humpty cried.

"I have not!" Alice said gently. "It's in a book."

"Ah, well. They may write it in a *book*," Humpty Dumpty said. "But, I'm one that has spoken to a King, *I* am. And, to show you I'm not snobbish, you may shake hands with me!"

And he grinned almost from ear to ear as he leaned forward and offered Alice his hand. She watched him nervously as she took it. "If he smiled much more, the ends of his mouth might meet behind his head," she thought, "and I'm afraid his head would come off!"

"Yes, all the King's horses and all his men," Humpty Dumpty went on. "They'd pick me up again in a minute, *they* would. However, this conversation is going on a little too fast. Let's go back to the next to the last remark."

"I'm afraid I can't quite remember it," Alice said very politely.

"In that case we start afresh, and it's my turn to choose a subject, so here's a question for you. How old did you say you were?"

Alice thought to herself for a moment, and said, "Seven years and six months."

"Wrong!" exclaimed Humpty Dumpty. "You never *said* how old you were!"

"I thought you meant 'How old *are* you?' " Alice explained.

"If I'd meant that, I'd have said it," said Humpty Dumpty.

Alice didn't want to argue, so she said nothing.

"Seven years and six months!" Humpty Dumpty repeated. "An uncomfortable sort of age. Now if you'd asked my advice, I'd have said 'Stop at seven'—but it's too late now."

"I never ask advice about growing," Alice said, but then she decided it was *her* turn to change the subject. "What a beautiful belt you've got on!"

"It's a cravat, child—a scarf—and a beautiful one, as you say. It's a present from the White King and Queen."

"Is it really?" said Alice.

Humpty Dumpty crossed one leg over the other. "They gave it to me for an un-birthday present."

"I beg your pardon?" Alice said. "What *is* an un-birthday present?"

"A present given when it isn't your birthday, of course."

Alice thought for a moment. "I like birthday presents best," she said at last.

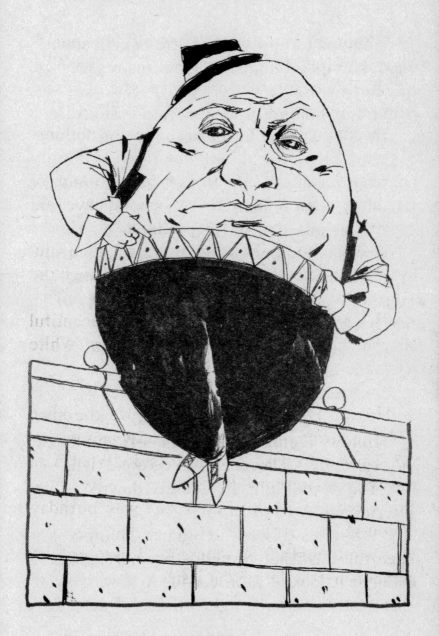

"You don't know what you're talking about!" cried Humpty Dumpty. "How many days are there in a year?"

"Three hundred and sixty-five," said Alice.

"And how many birthdays have you?"

"One."

"And if you take one from three hundred and sixty-five, what remains?"

"Three hundred and sixty-four, of course."

Humpty Dumpty looked at her doubtfully. "I'd like to see that done on paper," he said.

Alice couldn't help smiling as she took out her notebook, and worked the math for him:

$$\begin{array}{r} 365 \\ -\ 1 \\ \hline 364 \end{array}$$

Humpty Dumpty took the book, and looked at it carefully. "That seems to be done right—"

"You're holding it upside down!" Alice interrupted.

"Why, yes I was!" Humpty Dumpty said cheerfully, as Alice turned it around for him. "I thought it looked a little odd. As I was saying, that *seems* to be done right—though I don't have time to study it—and that shows that there are three hundred and sixty-four days when you might get un-birthday presents—"

"Certainly," said Alice.

"And only one for birthday presents, you know. There's glory for you!"

"I don't know what you mean by 'glory,' " said Alice.

Humpty Dumpty smiled smugly. "Of course you don't—till I tell you. I meant 'There's a nice knock-down argument for you.' "

"But 'glory' doesn't mean 'a nice knock-down argument,' " Alice objected.

"When *I* use a word," Humpty Dumpty said, "it means just what I choose it to mean—neither more nor less."

"You seem very clever at explaining words, sir," said Alice. "Would you kindly tell me the meaning of the poem called *Jabberwocky*?"

"Let's hear it," said Humpty Dumpty. "I can explain all the poems that ever were invented—and a good many that haven't been invented just yet."

This sounded very hopeful, so Alice repeated the first verse—

'Twas brillig, and the slithy toves
Did gyre and gimble in the wabe;
All mimsy were the borogoves,
And the mome raths outgrabe.

"That's enough to begin with," Humpty Dumpty interrupted. "There are plenty of hard words there. '*Brillig*' means four o'clock in the afternoon—the time when you begin *broiling* things for dinner."

"That'll do very well," said Alice. "And '*slithy*'?"

"Well, '*slithy*' means 'lithe and slimy.' 'Lithe' is the same as 'active.' You see it's like a two-sided suitcase—there are two meanings packed up into one word."

"I see it now," Alice remarked thoughtfully. "And what are '*toves*'?"

"Well, '*toves*' are something like badgers—they're something like lizards—and they're something like corkscrews."

"They must be very curious looking creatures," said Alice.

"They are that," said
Humpty Dumpty. "Also
they make their nests
under sundials—also
they live on cheese."
"And what's to '*gyre*'
and to '*gimble*'?"

"To '*gyre*' is
to go round and
round like a
gyroscope. To
'*gimble*' is to make
holes like a gimlet."

"And '*the wabe*' is the grassy area around a sundial, I suppose?" said Alice.

"Of course it is. It's called '*wabe*,' you know, because it goes a long way before it, and a long way behind it—"

"And a long way beyond it on each side," Alice added.

"Exactly so. Well, then, '*mimsy*' is 'flimsy and miserable' (there's another two-sided word for you). And a '*borogove*' is a thin shabby-looking bird with its feathers sticking out all round— something like a live mop."

"And then '*mome raths*'?" said Alice. "I'm afraid I'm giving you a great deal of trouble."

"Well, a '*rath*' is a sort of green pig, but '*mome*' I'm not certain about. I think it's short for 'from home'—meaning that they'd lost their way, you know."

"And what does '*outgrabe*' mean?"

"Well, '*outgrabing*' is something between bellowing and whistling, with a kind of sneeze in the middle. However, you'll hear it done, maybe—down in the woods yonder—and, when you've once heard it, you'll be *quite* content. Who's been repeating all that hard stuff to you?"

"I read it in a book," said Alice. "But I *had* some poetry repeated to me, much easier than that, by—Tweedledee, I think it was."

"As to poetry, you know," said Humpty Dumpty, stretching out one of his great hands, "*I* can repeat poetry as well as other folk, if it comes to that—"

"Oh, it doesn't need to come to *that*," said Alice.

But Humpty Dumpty went on to tell Alice a very long poem which she did not understand. It did, however, start to get interesting, Alice thought, as Humpty Dumpty said:

> "*And when I found the door was locked*
> *I pulled and pushed and kicked and knocked.*
> *And when I found the door was shut,*
> *I tried to turn the handle but—*"

But then there was a long pause.

"Is that all?" Alice timidly asked.

"That's all. Good-bye."

This was rather sudden, but Alice felt it wasn't right to stay. So she got up, and held out her hand. "Good-bye, until we meet again!" she said as cheerfully as she could.

"I wouldn't know you if we *did* meet again," Humpty Dumpty replied, giving her one of his fingers to shake. "You look just like other people."

"Most people try to remember the face," Alice suggested.

"That's just what I'm talking about," said Humpty Dumpty. "Your face is the same as everyone else's—the two eyes, nose in the middle, mouth under. It's always the same. Now if you had the two eyes on the same side of the nose, for instance—or the mouth at the top—that would be *some* help."

"It wouldn't look nice," Alice objected. But Humpty Dumpty only shut his eyes and said, "Wait till you've tried."

Alice waited a minute to see if he would speak again, but he never opened his eyes. "Good-bye!" she said once more, and quietly walked away.

She couldn't help saying to herself, "Of all the unsatisfactory—" (she repeated this out loud, for it was nice to say such a long word) "of all the unsatisfactory people I ever met—"

She never finished the sentence, for at this moment a heavy crash shook the forest from end to end.

CHAPTER SEVEN

The Lion and the Unicorn

The next moment, foot soldiers came running through the woods, at first in twos and threes, and then ten or twenty at a time. Then they seemed to fill the whole forest. Alice got behind a tree and watched them go by.

She had never seen soldiers so clumsy on their feet. They were always tripping over something and whenever one went down, several more always fell over him, so that the ground was soon covered with little heaps of men.

Then came the horses. Having four feet, these managed better than the soldiers, but even *they* stumbled now and then, and the riders fell off.

The confusion got worse every moment. Alice was very glad to get out of the woods into an open place, where she found the White King seated on the ground, busily writing in his notebook.

"I've sent them all!" the King cried in delight, on seeing Alice. "Did you happen to meet any soldiers, my dear, as you came through the woods?"

"Yes, I did," said Alice, "several thousand, I think."

"Four thousand two hundred and seven, that's the exact number," the King said, glancing at his notebook. "I couldn't send all the horses, you know, because two of them are needed in the chess game. And I didn't send the two Messengers, either. They've both gone to the town. Just look along the road and tell me if you can see either of them."

"I see nobody on the road," said Alice.

"I only wish I had such eyes," the King remarked. "To be able to see Nobody! And at that distance, too! Why, it's as much as I can do to see real people, by this light!"

"I see somebody now!" Alice exclaimed. "But he's coming very slowly—and moving around quite curiously!"

The Messenger, who looked like a hare, kept skipping up and down, wriggling like an eel as he came along, with his great hands spread out like fans on each side.

"Not at all," said the King. "He only does that when he's happy. His name is Haigha." (He pronounced it like "Hayer.") "The other Messenger is called Hatta. I must have *two*, you know—to come and go. One to come, and one to go."

"I beg your pardon?" said Alice.

"It isn't respectable to beg," said the King.

"I only meant that I didn't understand," said Alice. "Why one to come and one to go?"

"Didn't I tell you? I must have *two*—to fetch and carry. One to fetch, and one to carry."

At this moment the Messenger arrived. He was too out of breath to say a word, and could only wave his hands around, and make the most fearful faces at the poor King.

"This young lady is Alice," the King said. "And your silly looks are making me nervous! I feel faint—Give me a ham sandwich!"

The Messenger opened a bag that hung round his neck, and handed a sandwich to the King, who ate it up quickly.

"Another sandwich!" said the King.

"There's nothing but hay left now," the Messenger said, peeping into the bag.

"Hay, then," the King said in a faint whisper.

Alice was glad to see *that* pepped him up a great deal. "There's nothing like eating hay when you're faint," he said to her, as he munched away.

"I would think throwing cold water over you would be better," Alice suggested.

"I didn't say there was nothing *better*," the King replied. "I said there was nothing *like* it." The King turned to the Messenger and asked, "Whom did you pass on the road?"

"Nobody," said the Messenger.

"Quite right," said the King. "This young lady saw him, too. So of course Nobody walks slower than you."

"I do my best," the Messenger said. "I'm sure nobody walks much faster than I do!"

"He can't do that," said the King, "or else he'd have been here first. However, now you've got your breath, you may tell us what's happened in the town."

"I'll whisper it," said the Messenger, putting his hands to his mouth in the shape of a trumpet,

and stooping so as to get close to the King's ear.
Alice was sorry for this, for she wanted to hear the
news, too. However, instead of whispering, the
Messenger simply shouted at the top of his voice,
"They're at it again!"

"Do you call *that* a whisper?" cried the poor
King, jumping up and shaking himself. "If you
do such a thing again, I'll have you buttered!"

"Who are at it again?" Alice asked.

"Why, the Lion and the Unicorn, of course,"
said the King.

"Fighting for the crown?"

"Yes," said the King, "and the best of the joke
is that it's *my* crown! Let's run and see them."
And they trotted off, Alice repeating to herself, as
she ran, the words of the old song:

> *The Lion and the Unicorn*
> *were fighting for the crown.*
> *The Lion beat the Unicorn*
> *all around the town.*
> *Some gave them white bread,*
> *some gave them brown;*
> *Some gave them plum cake*
> *and drummed them out of town.*

"Does—the one—that wins—get the crown?" she asked, quite out of breath.

"Dear me, no!" said the King. "What an idea!"

"Would you—be good enough," Alice panted, "to stop a minute so I can catch my breath?"

"I'm *good* enough," the King said, "only I'm not *strong* enough to stop a minute. You see a minute goes by so very quick—you might as well try to stop a Bandersnatch."

Alice had no more breath for talking, so they trotted on in silence until they came in sight of a great crowd. In the middle of the crowd, the Lion and Unicorn were fighting.

They went over to where Hatta, the other Messenger, was standing watching the fight, with a cup of tea in one hand and a piece of bread-and-butter in the other.

"He's just out of prison," Haigha whispered to Alice, "and he hadn't finished his tea when he was sent in."

"How are they getting on with the fight?" asked the King.

Hatta swallowed quickly, and nearly choked. "They're getting on very well. Each of them has been down about eighty-seven times."

"Then I suppose they'll bring the white bread and the brown around soon?" Alice remarked.

"It's waiting for 'em now," said Hatta. "This is a bit of it that I'm eating."

There was a pause in the fight just then, and the Lion and the Unicorn sat down, panting, while the King called out, "Ten minutes allowed for refreshments!" Haigha and Hatta went to work at once, carrying trays of white and brown bread. Alice took a piece to taste, but it was *very* dry.

"I don't think they'll fight any more today," the King said to Hatta. "Go and order the drums to begin." And Hatta went bounding away like a grasshopper.

Just then, the Unicorn walked by them with his hands in his pockets. "I had the best of it this time, didn't I?" he asked the King, just glancing at him as he passed.

"A little—a little," the King replied nervously. "You shouldn't have run him through with your horn, you know."

"It didn't hurt him," the Unicorn said, and as he spoke, his eye fell on Alice. He turned around instantly and stood for some time staring at her.

"What—is—this?" he said at last.

"This is a child!" Haigha replied eagerly, stepping forward. "We only found it today."

"I always thought they were fabulous monsters!" said the Unicorn. "Is it alive?"

"It can talk," said Haigha solemnly.

The Unicorn looked dreamily at Alice, and said, "Talk, child."

Alice could not help her lips curling up into a smile as she began, "Do you know, I always thought Unicorns were fabulous monsters, too? I never saw one alive before!"

"Well, now that we *have* seen each other," said the Unicorn, "if you'll believe in me, I'll believe in you. Is that a bargain?"

"Yes," said Alice.

"Come, fetch out some plum cake, old man!" the Unicorn said to the King. "None of your brown bread for me!"

"Certainly—certainly!" the King muttered, and waved Haigha over. "Open the bag!" he whispered. "Quick! Not that one—that's full of hay!"

Haigha took a large cake out of the bag, and gave it to Alice to hold, while he got out a dish and carving knife. How they all came out of the bag Alice couldn't guess. It was like a magic trick.

The Lion had joined them while this was going on. He looked very tired and sleepy, and his eyes were half shut. "What's this!" he said, blinking lazily at Alice.

"Ah, you'll never guess!" the Unicorn cried eagerly. "*I* couldn't."

The Lion looked at Alice wearily. "Are you animal—vegetable—or mineral?" he said, yawning at every other word.

"It's a fabulous monster!" the Unicorn cried out, before Alice could reply.

"Then, hand out the plum cake, Monster," the Lion said, lying down and putting his chin on his paws. "And sit down, both of you," (to the King and the Unicorn). "Divide the cake fairly, now."

The King was evidently very uncomfortable at having to sit down between the two great creatures, but there was no other place for him.

"What a fight we might have for the crown, *now*!" the Unicorn said, looking at the King's crown. The poor King was nearly shaking it off his head, he trembled so much.

"I should win easy," said the Lion.

"I'm not so sure of that," said the Unicorn.

"Why, I beat you all around the town, you

chicken!" the Lion replied angrily, starting to get up as he spoke.

Here the King interrupted, to prevent the quarrel going on. He was very nervous, and his voice quivered. "All around the town?" he said. "That's a good long way. Did you go by the old bridge, or the marketplace? You get the best view by the old bridge."

"I don't know," the Lion growled as he lay down again. "There was too much dust to see anything. What a long time the Monster is taking, cutting up that cake!"

Alice had seated herself on the bank of a little brook with the dish on her knees, and was cutting the plum cake with the knife. "It's very frustrating!" she said, in reply to the Lion. "I've cut several slices already, but they join right back to the cake—it doesn't look sliced at all!"

"You don't know how to manage Looking Glass cakes," the Unicorn remarked. "Hand it around first, and cut it afterward."

This sounded nonsense, but Alice carried the dish around, and the cake divided itself into three pieces as she did so. "*Now* cut it up," said the Lion.

"I say, this isn't fair!" cried the Unicorn, as Alice sat, quite puzzled, with the knife in her hand. "The Monster has given the Lion twice as much as me!"

"She's kept none for herself, anyhow," said the Lion. "Do you like plum cake, Monster?"

But before Alice could answer him, the drums began. She couldn't tell where the noise came from, but the air seemed full of it. It rang through and through her head until she felt quite deafened. She got to her feet and sprang across the little brook in her terror—

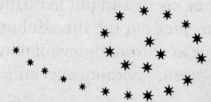

—and had just enough time to see the Lion and the Unicorn rise to their feet (with angry looks at being interrupted in their feast) before she dropped to her knees and put her hands over her ears, trying to shut out the dreadful uproar.

"If *that* doesn't 'drum them out of town,'" she thought to herself, "nothing ever will!"

CHAPTER EIGHT

"It's My Own Invention"

After a while the noise seemed to fade away, and Alice lifted up her head. There was no one to be seen. At first she thought she must have been dreaming about the Lion and the Unicorn and those odd Messengers. But there was the plum cake dish still lying at her feet, "So I wasn't dreaming, after all," she said to herself.

A loud shouting of "Ahoy! Ahoy! Check!" interrupted her thoughts and a Knight dressed in red armor came galloping up to her. Just as he reached her, the horse stopped suddenly. "You're my prisoner!" the Knight cried, as he tumbled off his horse.

Startled as she was, Alice was more frightened for *him* than for herself at the moment. She watched him as he jumped back onto his horse. As soon as he was comfortably in the saddle, he began once more, "You're my—" but here another voice broke in "Ahoy! Ahoy! Check!" and Alice looked around in some surprise for the new enemy.

This time it was a White Knight. He came to Alice's side, and tumbled off his horse just as the Red Knight had done. Then he got on again, and the two Knights sat and looked at each other for some time without speaking. Alice looked from one to the other with some bewilderment.

"She's *my* prisoner, you know!" the Red Knight said at last.

"Yes, but then *I* came and rescued her!" the White Knight replied.

"Well, we must fight for her, then," said the Red Knight, as he took up his helmet and put it on.

"You will follow the Rules of Battle, of course?" the White Knight said, putting on his helmet, too.

"I always do," said the Red Knight.

They began banging away at each other with such fury that Alice got behind a tree to be out of the way of the blows.

"I wonder what the Rules of Battle are," Alice said to herself as she watched the fight, peeping out from her hiding place. "One Rule seems to be that if one Knight hits the other, he knocks him off his horse—and if he misses, he tumbles off himself. Another Rule seems to be that they hold their clubs with their arms, as if they were Punch and Judy puppets. What noise when they tumble!"

Another Rule of Battle, that Alice had not noticed, seemed to be that they always fell on their heads. The battle ended with both falling off in this way, side by side. When they got up again, they shook hands, and then the Red Knight mounted and galloped off.

"It was a glorious victory, wasn't it?" said the White Knight, as he came up panting.

"I don't know," Alice said. "I don't want to be anybody's prisoner. I want to be a Queen."

"So you will, when you've crossed the next brook," said the White Knight. "I'll see you safe to the end of the woods—and then I must go back, you know. That's the end of my move."

"Thank you very much," said Alice. "May I help you off with your helmet?" It was more than *he* could handle, but she shook him out of it at last.

"Now I can breathe more easily," said the Knight, pulling back his shaggy hair. He turned his gentle face and large mild eyes to Alice. She had never seen such a strange-looking soldier in all her life.

He was dressed in tin armor, which fit him very badly, and he had an odd-shaped little pine box fastened across his shoulders, upside-down, and with the lid hanging open. Alice looked at it with great curiosity.

"I see you're admiring my little box," the Knight said in a friendly tone. "It's my own invention—to keep clothes and sandwiches in. You see I carry it upside-down, so that the rain can't get in."

"But the things can get *out*," Alice said gently. "Do you know the lid's open?"

"I didn't know it," the Knight said. "Then all the things must have fallen out! And the box is no use without them." He unfastened it as he spoke, and was just going to throw it into the bushes, when a thought seemed to strike him and he hung it carefully on a tree. "Can you guess why I did that?" he said to Alice.

Alice shook her head.

"In hopes some bees may make a nest in it—then I could get the honey."

"But you've got a beehive fastened to the saddle," said Alice.

"Yes, it's a very good beehive," the Knight said, "one of the best kind. But not a single bee has come near it yet. And the other thing is a mousetrap. I suppose the mice keep the bees out—or the bees keep the mice out, I don't know which."

"I was wondering what the mousetrap was for," said Alice. "It isn't very likely there would be any mice on the horse's back."

"Not very likely, perhaps," said the Knight. "But if they *do* come, I don't choose to have them running all about.

"You see," he went on after a pause, "it's good to be prepared for *everything*. That's the reason the horse has all those anklets round his feet."

"But what are they for?" Alice asked in a tone of great curiosity.

"To guard against the bites of sharks," the Knight replied. "It's an invention of my own. And now help me on. I'll go with you to the end of the woods—what's that dish for?"

"It's for plum cake," said Alice.

"We'd better take it with us," the Knight said. "It'll come in handy if we find any plum cake. Help me to get it into this bag."

This took a very long time to manage, though Alice held the bag open very carefully. The Knight was so *very* awkward in putting in the dish. The first two or three times that he tried he fell in himself instead. "It's rather a tight fit, you see," he said, as they got it in at last. "There are so many candlesticks in the bag." And he hung it to the saddle, which was already loaded with bunches of carrots, and fire irons, and many other things.

"I hope you've got your hair well fastened on?" he continued, as they set off.

"Only in the usual way," Alice said, smiling.

"That's hardly enough," he said anxiously. "You see, the wind is so *very* strong here—it's as strong as soup."

Alice puzzled over this and walked on in silence. Every now and then she would stop to help the poor Knight, who was *not* a good rider.

Whenever the horse stopped (which it did often), he fell off in front. And when it went on again, he fell off the back. And every now and then, he would fall off sideways.

"You've not had much practice in riding, I'm afraid," Alice said, as she was helping him up from his fifth tumble.

"What makes you say that?" he asked, as he scrambled back into the saddle, holding onto Alice's hair with one hand to save himself from falling over on the other side.

"Because people don't fall off quite so often when they've had much practice."

"I've had plenty of practice," the Knight said gravely. "Plenty of practice!" he kept repeating all the time Alice was getting him on his feet again.

"It's ridiculous!" cried Alice, losing all her patience as he tumbled once again. "You ought to have a wooden horse on wheels!"

"Does that kind go smoothly?" asked the Knight with great interest. He clasped his arms round the horse's neck as he spoke, just in time to save himself from tumbling off again.

"Much more smoothly than a live horse," Alice said, with a little scream of laughter.

"I'll get one," the Knight said thoughtfully to himself. "One or two—several."

"What a curious helmet you've got!" Alice remarked. "Is that your own invention, too?"

The Knight looked down proudly at his helmet, which hung from the saddle. "Yes," he said, "but I've invented a better one than that. It was quite large, so when I fell off the horse, it touched the ground first and I had a *very* little way to fall, you see—but there *was* always the danger of falling *into* it. That happened to me once—and before I could get out again, the other White Knight came and put it on. He thought it was his own helmet."

"Did you hurt him," Alice asked, trying not to giggle, "being on the top of his head?"

"I had to kick him, of course," the Knight said very seriously. "And then he took the helmet off again—but it took hours and hours to get me out."

He raised his hands in some excitement as he said this, and instantly rolled out of the saddle, and fell headlong into a deep ditch.

Alice ran to the side of the ditch to look for him. She was startled by the fall, and was afraid that he really *was* hurt this time. She could see nothing but the soles of his feet, but was relieved to hear that he was talking on in his usual tone.

"How *can* you go on talking with your head downward?" Alice asked, as she dragged him out by the feet, and laid him in a heap on the bank.

The Knight looked surprised at the question. "What does it matter where my body happens to be?" he said. "My mind goes on working all the same."

They walked on until they had come to the end of the woods. The White Knight announced, "And here I must leave you. You've only a few yards to go, down the hill and over that little brook, and then you'll be a Queen—but you'll stay and see me off first?" he added as Alice turned to look eagerly for the brook. "I shan't be long. You'll wait and wave your handkerchief when I get to that turn in the road? It will encourage me, you see."

"Of course I'll wait," said Alice. "And thank you very much for coming so far."

So they shook hands, and then the Knight rode slowly away into the forest. "It won't take long to see him *off*, I expect," Alice said to herself, as she stood watching him. "There he goes! Right on his head as usual!" She watched as the Knight tumbled off, first on one side and then on the other. After the fourth or fifth tumble he reached the turn. Then she waved her handkerchief to him, and waited until he was out of sight.

"I hope it encouraged him," she said, as she turned to run down the hill. "And now for the last brook, and to be a Queen! How grand it sounds!"

A very few steps brought her to the edge of the brook. "The Eighth Square at last!" she cried as she ran across—

—and threw herself down on a flowered lawn.

"Oh, how glad I am to get here! And what *is* this on my head?" she exclaimed, as she put her hands up to something very heavy that fitted tight all around her head.

"But how *can* it have got there without my knowing it?" she said to herself, as she lifted it off, and set it on her lap to figure out what it was.

It was a golden crown.

CHAPTER NINE

Queen Alice

"Well, this *is* grand!" said Alice. "I never expected I would be a Queen so soon."

Alice got up and walked around—rather stiffly at first, for fear of the crown falling. "If I really *am* a Queen," she said as she sat down again, "I will be able to manage it in time."

She wasn't a bit surprised to find the Red Queen and the White Queen sitting close to her, one on each side. She wanted to ask them how they came there, but she feared it would not be polite. Surely there would be no harm in asking if the game was over. "Please, would you tell me—" she began, looking timidly at the Red Queen.

"Speak when you're spoken to!" the Red Queen said sharply.

"But if everybody obeyed that rule," said Alice, "nobody would ever say anything, so that—"

"Ridiculous!" interrupted the Queen. Then, after thinking for a minute, she asked, "What do you mean by 'If I really *am* a Queen'? You can't be a Queen, until you've passed the proper test. And the sooner we begin it, the better."

"I only said 'if'!" poor Alice pleaded.

The two Queens looked at each other, and the Red Queen remarked, with a little shudder, "She *says* she only said 'if'—"

"But she said a great deal more than that!" the White Queen moaned. "Oh, ever so much more."

"So you did, you know," the Red Queen said to Alice. "Always speak the truth—think before you speak—and write it down afterward."

There was an uncomfortable silence for a minute or two.

The Red Queen broke the silence by saying to the White Queen, "I invite you to Alice's dinner party this afternoon."

The White Queen smiled feebly, and said, "And I invite *you*."

"I didn't know I was to have a party at all," said Alice, "but if there *is* to be one, I think *I* ought to invite the guests."

"We gave you the opportunity of doing it," the Red Queen remarked, "but you've not had many lessons in manners yet?"

"Manners are not taught in lessons," said Alice. "Lessons teach you to do sums, and things like that."

"Can you do Addition?" the White Queen asked. "What's one and one and one and one and one and one and one and one and one and one?"

"I don't know," said Alice. "I lost count."

"She can't do Addition," the Red Queen interrupted. "Can you do Subtraction? Take nine from eight."

"Nine from eight? I can't," Alice replied, "but—"

"She can't do Subtraction," said the White Queen. "Can you do Division? Divide a loaf by a knife—what's the answer to *that*?"

"I suppose—" Alice was beginning, but the Red Queen answered for her. "Bread-and-butter, of course."

Alice couldn't help thinking to herself, "What nonsense we *are* talking!"

෨ 158 ෨

"She can't do sums a *bit*!" said both Queens at the same time.

"Can *you* do sums?" Alice said, turning suddenly on the White Queen.

The Queen gasped and shut her eyes. "I can do Addition," she said, "if you give me time—but I can't do Subtraction under *any* circumstances!"

"I wish Queens never asked questions," Alice thought to herself.

Then the White Queen said, "What is the cause of lightning?"

"The cause of lightning," Alice said, "is the thunder—no, no!" she quickly corrected herself. "I meant the other way around."

"It's too late to correct it," said the Red Queen. "Once you've said a thing, that fixes it, and you must take the consequences."

"Which reminds me—" the White Queen said, looking down and nervously clasping and unclasping her hands, "we had *such* a thunderstorm last Tuesday—I mean one of the last set of Tuesdays."

Alice was confused. "In *our* country," she remarked, "there's only one day at a time."

The Red Queen said, "That's a poor way of doing things. *Here*, we mostly have days and nights two or three at a time, and sometimes in the winter we have as many as five nights together—for five times the warmth, you know."

Alice sighed at such nonsense.

The White Queen began again. "It was *such* a thunderstorm, you can't think! And part of the roof came off, and so much thunder got in—and it went rolling around the room in great lumps—and knocking over the tables and things—until I was so frightened, I couldn't remember my own name!"

"Your Majesty must excuse her," said the Red Queen to Alice. The Red Queen took one of the White Queen's hands in her own. "She means well, but she can't help saying foolish things. She was never really well brought up. A little kindness and putting her hair in curlers would do wonders for her."

The White Queen gave a deep sigh, and laid her head on Alice's shoulder. "I *am* so sleepy," she moaned.

"She's tired, poor thing!" said the Red Queen. "Smooth her hair—lend her your nightcap—and sing her a soothing lullaby."

"I haven't got a nightcap with me," said Alice, as she tried to obey the first direction, "and I don't know any soothing lullabies."

"I must do it myself, then," said the Red Queen, and she began:

"Hush-a-by lady, in Alice's lap!
Till the feast's ready, we've time for a nap.
When the feast's over, we'll go to the ball—
Red Queen, and White Queen, and Alice, and all!

"And now you know the words," she added, as she put her head down on Alice's other shoulder, "sing it to *me*. I'm getting sleepy, too." Soon both Queens were fast asleep, and snoring loud.

"What *am* I to do?" exclaimed Alice, looking around as one of the heads—then the other—rolled down from her shoulder and into her lap.

"Do wake up!" she said. There was no answer but a gentle snoring.

The snoring seemed to have a rhythm, and was sounding more like a tune. At last she could even hear words. She started to listen closely, when the two great heads suddenly vanished from her lap.

Alice found herself standing before an arched doorway with the words "QUEEN ALICE" written in large letters. On each side of the arch there was a bell handle. One was marked "Visitors' Bell," and the other "Servants' Bell."

"I'll wait till the song's over," thought Alice, "and then I'll ring—the—the—*which* bell must I ring? I'm not a visitor, and I'm not a servant. There *ought* to be one marked 'Queen,' you know."

Just then the door opened a little way. A creature with a long beak put its head out for a moment and said, "No admittance until the week after next!" and shut the door again with a bang.

Alice knocked and rang for a long time. At last a very old Frog, who was sitting under a tree, got up and hobbled toward her. He was dressed in bright yellow and had enormous boots on.

"You shouldn't knock at the door," he muttered. "Shouldn't do that—shouldn't do that. It bothers it, you know." Then he gave the door a kick with one of his great feet. "You let *it* alone," he panted as he hobbled back, "and it'll let *you* alone, you know."

The door was flung open, and a shrill voice was heard singing:

To the Looking Glass world it was Alice that said,
"I've a scepter in hand, I've a crown on my head.
Let the Looking Glass creatures, whatever they be,
Come and dine with the Red Queen,
                                    the White Queen and me!"

And hundreds of voices joined in the chorus:

Then fill up the glasses as quick as you can,
And sprinkle the table with buttons and bran.
Put cats in the coffee, and mice in the tea—
And welcome Queen Alice with thirty-times-three!

"I'd better go in at once—" thought Alice. In she went, and there was a dead silence the moment she appeared.

Alice glanced nervously along the table as she walked up the large dining hall, and noticed that there were about fifty guests of all kinds. Some were animals, some were birds, and there were even a few flowers among them.

There were three chairs at the head of the table. The Red and White Queens had already taken two of them, but the middle one was empty. Alice sat down in it, rather uncomfortable at the silence, and longing for someone to speak.

At last the Red Queen began. "You've missed the soup and fish," she said. "Put on the leg!" And the waiters set a leg of mutton before Alice, who looked at it rather sheepishly, as she had never had to carve a leg of mutton before.

"You look a little shy. Let me introduce you to that leg of mutton," said the Red Queen. "Alice—Leg of Mutton. Leg of Mutton—Alice." The leg got up in the dish and made a little bow to Alice. Alice returned the bow, not knowing whether to be frightened or amused.

"May I give you a slice?" she said, taking up the knife and fork.

"Certainly not," the Red Queen said. "It isn't good manners to cut anyone you've been introduced to. Remove the leg!" And the waiters carried it off, and brought a large loaf of plum pudding in its place.

"Please don't introduce me to the plum pudding," Alice said quickly, "or we shall get no dinner at all. May I give you some?"

But the Red Queen growled, "Pudding—Alice. Alice—Pudding. Remove the pudding!" and the waiters took it away so quickly that Alice couldn't return its bow.

Alice didn't see why the Red Queen should be the only one to give orders, so, as an experiment, she called out, "Waiter! Bring back the pudding!" and there it was again, like magic. She cut a slice and handed it to the Red Queen.

"How rude!" said the Pudding. "I wonder how you'd like it if I were to cut a slice out of *you*, you creature!"

It spoke in a thick sort of voice, and Alice could only look at it and gasp.

"Make a remark," said the Red Queen. "It's ridiculous to leave all the conversation to the pudding! Take a minute to think about what you're going to say. Meanwhile, we'll drink to your health—to Queen Alice's health!" she screamed at the top of her voice, and all the guests began drinking in all sorts of odd ways. "Give your thanks in a neat speech," the Red Queen said to Alice.

"We will support you," the White Queen whispered as Alice got up.

"Thank you very much," Alice whispered in reply, "but I can do quite well without your support."

"That won't do at all," the Red Queen said. So Alice let them support her.

The two Queens pushed her so, one on each side, that they nearly lifted her up into the air. "I rise to return thanks—" Alice began—and she really *did* rise as she spoke, several inches, but she grabbed the edge of the table and managed to pull herself down again.

"Take care of yourself!" screamed the White Queen, grabbing Alice's hair with both her hands. "Something's going to happen!"

And then all sorts of things *did* happen. The candles all grew up to the ceiling, looking something like a bed of rushes with fireworks at the top. The bottles each took a pair of plates, which they fitted on as wings, and, with forks for legs, went fluttering about in all directions. "They looked very much like birds," Alice thought.

She heard a laugh at her side, and turned to see what was the matter with the White Queen. But instead of the Queen, there was the leg of mutton sitting in the chair. "Here I am!" cried a voice from the soup pot, and Alice turned again, just in time to see the Queen's face grinning at her over the edge of the pot, before she disappeared into the soup.

There was not a moment to be lost. Already several of the guests were lying down in the dishes, and the soup ladle was walking up the table toward Alice's chair, and motioning to her to get out of its way.

"I can't stand this any longer!" Alice cried as she jumped up and seized the tablecloth with both hands. One good pull—and plates, dishes, guests, and candles came crashing down together in a heap on the floor.

"And as for *you*—" she went on, turning upon the Red Queen (who surely was the cause of all the mischief). But the Queen was no longer at her side—she had suddenly dwindled down to the size of a little doll, and was now on the table, merrily running around and around after her own shawl, which was trailing behind her.

"As for *you*," she repeated, picking the Red Queen up, "I'll shake you into a kitten—that I will!"

CHAPTER TEN

Shaking

She took her off the table as she spoke and shook her backward and forward.

The Red Queen put up no fuss whatsoever, only her face grew very small, and her eyes got large and green. And still, as Alice went on shaking her, she kept on growing shorter—and fatter—and softer—and rounder—and—

Waking

—and it really *was* a kitten, after all.

Which Dreamed It?

"Your Red Majesty shouldn't purr so loud," Alice said, rubbing her eyes, talking to the kitten. "You woke me out of oh! such a nice dream! You've been with me all along, Kitty—all through the Looking Glass world. Do you remember?"

The kitten only purred—and it was impossible to guess whether it meant "yes" or "no."

Alice hunted among the chessmen on the table until she had found the Red Queen. Then she went down on her knees on the hearth rug, and put the kitten and the Queen so they could look at each other. "Now, Kitty!" she cried. "Confess that you turned into the Red Queen!"

"Snowdrop, my pet!" she went on, looking over her shoulder at the White Kitten. It was still being washed by Dinah, the mother cat. "That must be the reason you were so untidy in my dream." She turned back to the black kitten. "By the way, Kitty, if only you'd really been with me in my dream, there was one thing you *would* have enjoyed—I had quite a bit of poetry said to me. Tomorrow morning you shall have a real treat. All the time you're eating your breakfast, I'll repeat *The Walrus and the Carpenter* to you—and then you can make believe it's oysters, dear!

"Now, Kitty, who was it that dreamed it all? You see, Kitty, it *must* have been either me or the Red King. He was part of my dream—but then I was part of his dream, too! *Was* it the Red King, Kitty? You were his wife, so you ought to know— Oh, Kitty, *do* help to settle it!" But the kitten only licked its paw, and pretended it hadn't heard the question.

Which do *you* think it was?

THE END

ABOUT THE AUTHOR

LEWIS CARROLL

Charles Lutwidge Dodgson (Lewis Carroll) was born in 1832, one of eleven children of a country parson. He was a very bright child and student, but he stuttered and this bothered him all his life. He attended college at Oxford, went on to teach mathematics there, was ordained as a minister, and remained at Oxford the rest of his life.

Although he was snobbish, cranky, and stern, children liked him and he adored children. In 1862, he took several people, including three daughters of a college dean, out on a boat trip, where they were caught in a rainstorm. Later, Alice, the middle daughter, asked Dodgson to tell a story. He made up a funny tale about Alice and some animals in a pool of tears. This was the start of *Alice's Adventures in Wonderland*, which Dodgson published under the name of Lewis Carroll in 1865.

The book was a sensation. As Lewis Carroll, Dodgson added to Alice's adventures in 1871 with *Through the Looking Glass*, introducing more unusual characters, poetry, and fanciful nonsense. He died in 1898. His books went on to change ideas about children's literature forever.